A Note to Parents

Read to your child...

★ Reading aloud is one of the best ways to develop your child's love of reading. Read together at least 20 minutes each day.

★ Laughter is contagious! Read with feeling. Show your child that reading is fun.

★ Take time to answer questions your child may have about the story. Linger over pages that interest your child.

...and your child will read to you.

★ Do not correct every word your child misreads. Instead, say, "Does that make sense? Let's try it again."

★ Praise your child as he progresses. Your encouraging words will build his confidence.

You can help your Level 2 reader.

★ Keep the reading experience interactive. Read part of a sentence, then ask your child to add the missing word.

★ Read the first part of a story. Then ask, "What's going to happen next?"

★ Give clues to new words. Say, "This word begins with *b* and ends in *ake*, like *rake, take, lake.*"

★ Ask your child to retell the story using her own words.

★ Use the five *W*s: WHO is the story about? WHAT happens? WHERE and WHEN does the story take place? WHY does it turn out the way it does?

Most of all, enjoy your reading time together!

—Bernice Cullinan, Ph.D.,
Professor of Reading, New York University

Published by Reader's Digest Children's Books
Reader's Digest Road, Pleasantville, NY U.S.A. 10570-7000

10 9 8

Library of Congress Cataloging-in-Publication Data

Schade, Susan.
Dinosaur Ed / by Susan Schade and Jon Buller.
p. cm. — (All-star readers. Level 2)
Summary: A dinosaur figures out how to make his sled work when there's no snow.
ISBN 1-57584-385-4 (alk. paper)
[1. Dinosaurs Fiction. 2. Building Fiction. 3. Stories in rhyme.]
I. Buller, Jon, ill. II. Title. III. Series.
PZ8.3.S287Di 2000 [E]—dc21 99-37416

Dinosaur Ed

by Susan Schade
and Jon Buller

Reader's Digest Children's Books™
Pleasantville, New York • Montréal, Québec

Dinosaur Ed
gets out of bed.

He gets his socks.

He chews some rocks.

His teeth are clean.

His shorts are green.

He has a shelf
he made himself.

He also made
a lamp and shade,

a cup and bowl,

a fishing pole,

two stools,

his bed,

and this red sled!

The sun is high.
The ground is dry.

There is no snow.
The sled won't go.

Ed sees his stools.

He gets his tools.

He chips off bits.

He drills.

He splits.

Four wheels on poles,

and Ed's sled rolls.

Now Ed can go

on dirt . . .

or . . .

snow!

Words are fun!

Here are some simple activities you can do with a pencil, crayons, and a sheet of paper. You'll find the answers at the bottom of the page.

★

1. Find a word in the story that means the opposite of:

low	**in**
wet	**stop**
dirty	**yes**

2. Circle the two words in each line that rhyme.

rock	**shade**	**sock**
shelf	**bed**	**red**
stool	**lamp**	**tool**
bowl	**ground**	**roll**
dirt	**snow**	**go**
high	**dry**	**sled**

3. If you could build something with wheels to ride in, what would it be? Draw a picture.

4. How much of the story do you remember? Choose the word that correctly completes the sentence.

a. Dinosaur Ed's shorts are
purple **dirty** **green**

b. Dinosaur Ed made a
cake **shelf** **rocket**

c. Dinosaur Ed gets out of a
bed **bath** **tent**

d. Dinosaur Ed's sled
flies **rolls** **jumps**

e. Dinosaur Ed wears
socks **a shirt** **a coat**

f. Dinosaur Ed fixes his sled with
cookies **crayons** **tools**

ANSWERS:
1. low/high; wet/dry; dirty/clean; in/out; stop/go; yes/no
2. rock=sock; bed=red; stool=tool; bowl=roll; snow=go; high=dry
4. a. green; b. shelf; c. bed; d. rolls; e. socks; f. tools